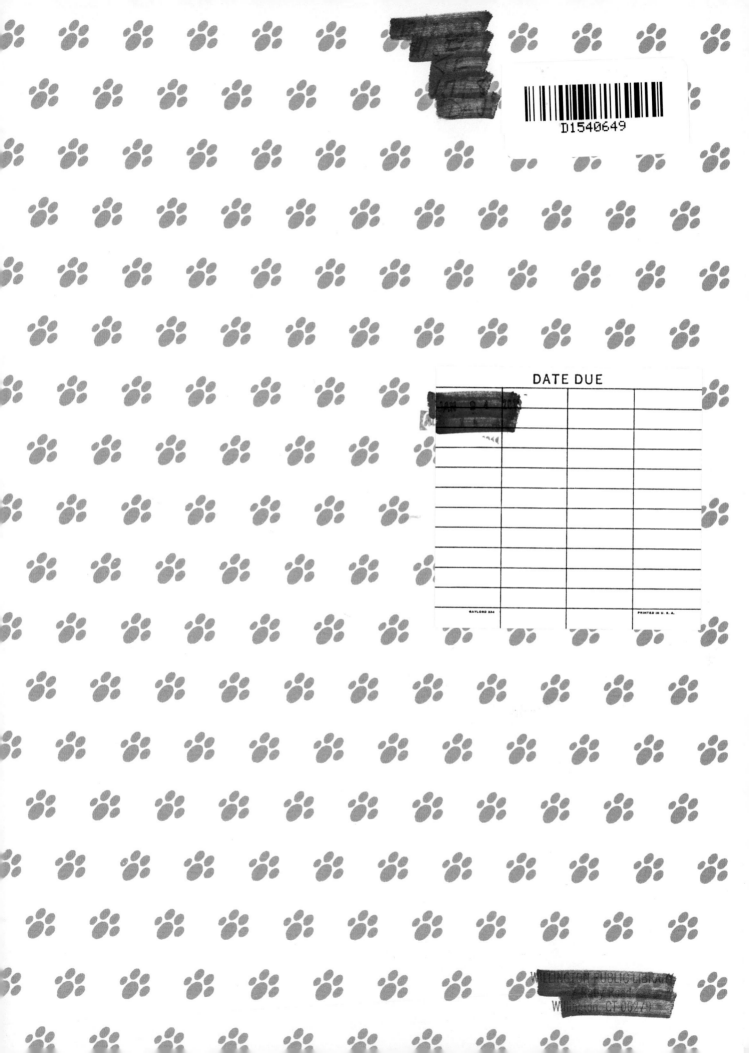

GARFIELD

LEARNS ABOUT THOUGHTFULNESS
Don't Be Late!

Created by Jim Davis

Story by Mark Acey

Illustrated by Paws, Inc.

A GOLDEN BOOK • NEW YORK

Western Publishing Company, Inc.
Racine, Wisconsin 53404

Late one morning Garfield was watching his favorite game show, "Bowling for Donuts," when he heard a knock at the door.

"Drat! Just when he's going for the jumbo danish," grumbled Garfield as he stormed across the room and threw open the door.

SPLUT!

A pie splattered in Garfield's face.

"Bon appetit," said Arlene angrily.

"Mmmm…banana cream…one of my favorites," said Garfield as he licked his lips. "What did I do to deserve home delivery?"

"That's your 'just desserts' for missing our dinner date last night," snapped Arlene. "I went to a lot of trouble to prepare a special meal. And you didn't even bother to show up."

"When you eat as many meals as I do, it's easy to lose track," said Garfield. "Could we try again tonight?"

"A rude cat like you doesn't deserve another chance!" Arlene turned and stomped away.

"I don't know why Arlene was so cranky," said Garfield.
"By now she should be used to me forgetting our dates."
Garfield checked his calendar.

"There's no record of any dinner with Arlene. Maybe I
should start writing these things down."

Suddenly there was another knock at the door.
"It's probably Arlene wanting to make up," thought
Garfield. "She's nuts about me."
Garfield eagerly opened the door.

DOINK!

"Hey, Jelly Belly, where were you last night?" asked Nermal. "You were supposed to videotape my rubber mouse juggling act for 'America's Cutest Kitties.'"

"Cute is overrated," replied Garfield. "Besides, you
must be mistaken. It seems I promised Arlene I'd have
dinner with her last night. I can't be in two places at once."

"Why not?" cracked Nermal. "You're certainly big
enough to try."

And with that, Nermal turned and stomped away.

Garfield was finally about to sit back down when he heard a loud crash outside the window. Seconds later Odie burst through the door.

"Let me guess," began Garfield. "I forgot to hold the ladder for you while you were washing the windows, right? Good thing that bucket cushioned your fall."

"Grrr!" growled Odie. He dumped the bucket over Garfield's head and stomped away.

"Like I said," muttered Garfield. "I've got to start writing things down. It would be a lot easier on my mind—not to mention my skull."

All that stress made Garfield sleepy. Of course, he was always sleepy.

"All my friends are mad at me, Pooky. They think I let them down. Thank goodness I still have you."

Garfield gave the little bear a great big hug.

"Friends may come and friends may go," thought
Garfield, "but a teddy bear is forever."
   Garfield placed Pooky beside his bed and soon was off
to sleep.

Later that afternoon, Garfield awoke from his nap. He reached over to hug Pooky, but to his astonishment and horror—*Pooky was gone!* In his place lay a mysterious piece of paper with a mysterious message:

WE HAVE YOUR BEAR. BRING TEN UNMARKED PIZZAS TO CORNWALL PARK TONIGHT AT 5 O'CLOCK
P.S. DON'T BE LATE!

"Bearnappers!" cried Garfield. "They've got my Pooky! What'll I do? What'll I do?"

Garfield took a deep breath.

"OK, stay calm…no need to panic. I'll just follow the bearnappers' instructions, and they'll return Pooky unharmed.

"All this stress has made me hungry," said Garfield. "Of course, I'm always hungry."

So Garfield whipped up a light snack.
"Nothing like a lasagna and fudge sundae to help
steady the nerves. And there's still plenty of time for me to
watch my favorite soap opera, 'One Life to Eat.'"

So Garfield settled into his chair. The next thing he knew, he had not only watched his favorite soap opera, but his favorite cartoons as well.

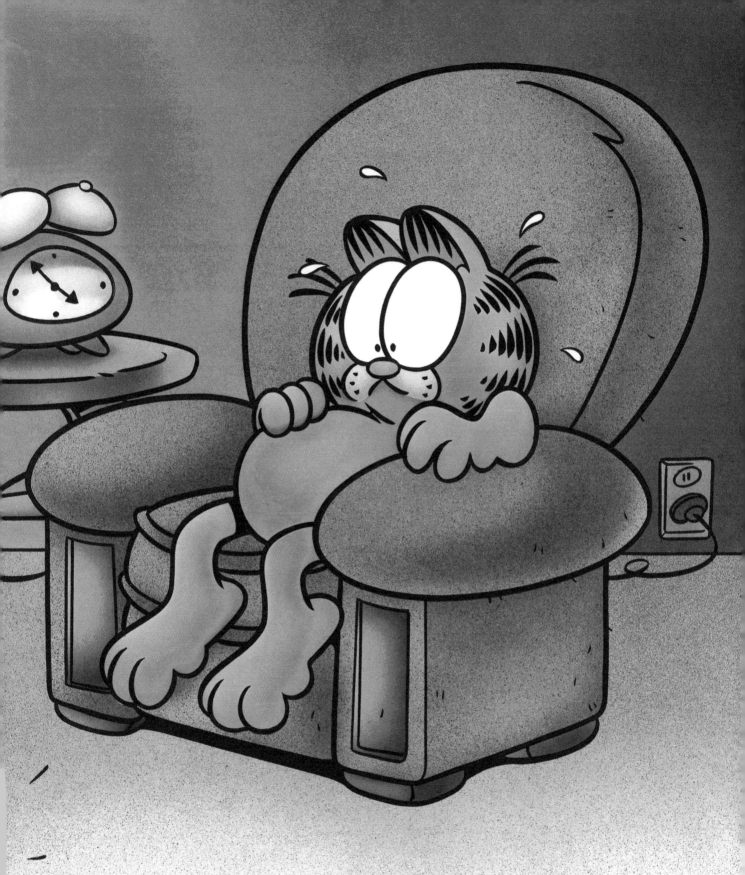

When the cartoons ended, Garfield glanced at the clock.
The little hand was on the five and the big hand was on
the eleven.

"Oh, no!" cried Garfield. "How did it get so late?"

Garfield panicked. He ran to the freezer to get the pizzas.

"Did they want five or ten—or was it fifteen? Oh, well…the more, the tastier. Hang on, Pooky! I'm coming!"

Garfield wobbled out the door, carrying the leaning tower of pizzas. Suddenly he stopped.

"Which park?" he thought. "Was it Limburger? Hindenburg? I know it wasn't Candlestick. Now I remember! It was Cornwall!!"

And with that, the pizza-packing fat cat staggered and stumbled his way to the park.

When he arrived, Garfield's worst fears were realized.
The park was empty—no bear and no bearnappers.

"Poor Pooky's been turned into a cushion!" sobbed Garfield. "People are going to sit on him. No-o-o-o! It's all my fault. If only I had been on time. If only I had been dependable!"

Just then, out popped Arlene, Nermal, and Odie.
"Looking for this?" asked Arlene.
"Pooky!" exclaimed Garfield. "You're OK! But where,
uh, what—HEY!—I know what's going on. You're the
bearnappers! Why you weasels, it's not nice to play tricks
like that!"

"It's also not nice to keep people waiting and disappoint your friends," replied Arlene. "If you say you're going to be someplace, you should be there—and be there on time. We wanted to teach you a lesson."

"You're right," admitted Garfield. "I guess I deserved it. I'm sorry. From now on I'll try to do better."

They all went back to Jon's for a "Welcome Home, Pooky" party.

"Lugging those pizzas around certainly made me hungry," said Garfield.

"Everything makes you hungry," chimed in Nermal.

"I know," replied Garfield. "That's one thing you can always depend on!"

Make Your Own Birthday Calendar

Garfield found out how easy it is to forget important dates if they aren't written down. Here's a simple way to keep track of birthdays. This same calendar can be used year after year.

You'll need:
2 pieces of white poster board
(oak tag), usually 22 inches by 28 inches
safety scissors
a pencil
a ruler
string or ribbon
a hole punch

Step 1: Draw a line down the middle of each poster board, dividing it into two halves, left and right. Then draw a line across the middle of each board, dividing it into two halves, top and bottom. Cut along these lines and you will end up with eight pieces, each 11 inches by 14 inches. You will use six of these pieces.

Step 2: Hold a piece of the poster board lengthwise and write the name of the first month, January, at the top. Each piece will show two months (front and back). December goes on the back of January, November on the back of February, October on the back of March, September on the back of April, August on the back of May, and July on the back of June.

Step 3: Using your ruler, draw one line across the sheet for each day of the month. Remember—April, June, September, and November have only thirty days. Use twenty-nine days for February. The remaining months all have thirty-one days. Each line should be 3/8 inch above the next. Write the dates on the left side of each line.

Step 4: Go through the year and write in the names of your friends or relatives next to their birthdays. Leave enough room for additional names.

Step 5: Put the six sheets in order (January to June) and punch a hole at the top in the center. Tie a string or ribbon through the hole and hang the birthday calendar on your wall. At the end of June, just turn all the sheets around and the second half of the year will be in correct order.